MARK TWAIN
THE MAMMOTH COD

"You would pluck out the heart
of my mystery."

—*Hamlet*, III. ii.

MALEDICTA PRESS PUBLICATIONS · I

GENERAL EDITOR: REINHOLD AMAN

THIS FIRST EDITION OF MARK TWAIN'S
THE MAMMOTH COD
AND OTHER WRITINGS, IS STRICTLY LIMITED.
THIS COPY IS NUMBERED:

MARK TWAIN

THE MAMMOTH COD

AND ADDRESS TO
THE STOMACH CLUB

WITH AN INTRODUCTION BY

G. LEGMAN

MALEDICTA
1976

MALEDICTA, INC.

3275 North Marietta Avenue
Milwaukee, Wisconsin 53211

Printed in the United States of America

CONTENTS

MARK TWAIN'S
MAMMOTH COD

MARK TWAIN'S erotic and scatological pieces, insofar as there is now any record of these, began with the endlessly-reprinted *"1601, or Conversation as it was by the Social Fireside in the Time of the Tudors"* (1st edition, 1880), written just a century ago, in 1876, during a pause between his two masterpieces, *The Adventures of Tom Sawyer* and *Huckleberry Finn,* at the height of his powers. This was followed by Twain's "Address to the Stomach Club of Paris, 1879: *Some Remarks on the Science of Onanism,"* first circulated by the Twain specialist, Franklin J. Meine, in typewritten copies during the 1940's, and by a Chicago advertising man, George Brownell, in twenty-five mimeographed copies circulated among members of the Mark Twain Society of Chicago in 1952. It was first actually printed in Ralph Ginzburg's *Fact* magazine (New York, March 1964) Vol. I, No. 2: pages 18-21, having been intended earlier for publication in the same editor's banned magazine, *Eros,* No. 5, which never appeared. This piece is given at the end of the present pamphlet, from one of the copies made by Meine from the original manuscript, then in the possession of Charles T. Lark, attorney for the Mark Twain estate.

In printing recently the most famous travesty oration now in folk-transmission in America, "Change the Name of Arkansaw?!" in *Rationale of the Dirty Joke: Second Series, "No Laughing Matter"* (1975) end of section 14.I.5, pages 755-58, under the heading "Mocking Authority-Figures," the present editor argues that this is also perhaps by Mark Twain, and is in a sense the true version of the expurgated contest in bombast and brag that precedes the fight on the raft in Twain's *Life on the Mississippi* (1883). This suggestion was apparently first broached by Miss Nancy Clemens—perhaps from inside knowledge?—in James R. Masterson's courageous *Tall Tales of Arkansaw* (Boston: Chapman & Grimes, 1942), which also first publicly printed the "Change the Name of Arkansaw?!" speech in the notes at the end of the book.

Certain Twain experts have taken the opposite position, and maintain that the violently dysphemistic Arkansaw speech is an obvious imitation, and that Twain's bragging-contest is the original. We will never know. The form, of the mock bombastic speech, is in any case ancient, dating from late medieval times, when such were often delivered by the burlesque Goliard poets during the irreligious "Feast of Fools." As for example the *Officium lusorum* or "Gamblers' Mass," *Carmina Burana,* No. 215.

By the mid-nineteenth century or before, mock speeches had become a standard form of humor in both England and America, as in the *Speech of Gen. Riley in the House of Representatives of Missouri,* printed in the *Hannibal Weekly Messenger,* March 7th, 1861, "excavated and edited" by Franklin J. Meine (Chicago: The Mark Twain Society of Chicago, 1940). The entirely serious patriotic orators of the same period were sometimes even funnier, as witness the perfectly incredible flights of bombast by Edwin H. Tenney, a Nashville attorney, at the 83rd anniversary of American Independence, July 4th, 1859, at Rome, Tennessee, reprinted in Edmund Lester Pearson's *Queer Books* (New York, 1928) chapter 2, "Making the Eagle Scream," pages

29-39, and 157-59, for history to wonder at. Mark Twain couldn't even approach the Hon. Edwin H. Tenney for true humor—alas, entirely unconscious.

As is not well known, Mark Twain also occasionally expressed himself in brief and sometimes bawdy verse, usually at a bit higher level than his "translation" into jingles of Dr. Heinrich Hoffmann's horrid sadistic picture-book for bad children, *Struwwelpeter,* as published by the First Edition Club. For example, the anthem or quatrain sung by the germs in the large intestine—their Heaven—in Letter VII of Twain's *Letters from the Earth* (posthumously published, New York, 1962) beginning "Constipation, O constipation." So also "The Mysterious Chinaman," a brief and not very humorous travesty of Edgar Allan Poe's "The Raven," preserved in the Yale University Library, Beinecke Rare Book and Manuscript Collection. This trifle was first published in *The Twainian* (July 1947, page 3), and is the low-point of Mark Twain's art.

Also unpublished hitherto are two brief stanzas noted in Prof. Arthur L. Scott's *On the Poetry of Mark Twain* (1966) page 36, as being patterned after FitzGerald's *Rubáiyát of Omar Khayyám,* which Twain sincerely loved. (Unpublished Mark Twain Papers, at the University of California, Berkeley: DW #23, now DV-200; and compare Notebook #38.) Notebook #38 also contains some off-color jokes and allusions, and a brief political invective in two quatrain stanzas, printed by Scott, page 36. This is very violent for Twain, beginning: "Ho, burghers of Dutch Albany, Ho, buggers of New York," and going on to state that no one will or should vote for William Randolph Hearst, the muckraking newspaper publisher then (1906) running for the governorship of New York, except gallows-birds and convicts, "sons of bitches from the slums, And painted whores from Cork."

MARK TWAIN

In the finished copy of this manuscript poem in the Beinecke
Collection at Yale, Twain notes, as to the whores from Cork, that this
is "A poetically-licensed divergence from fact. They don't come from
there." This copy also adds a full title and tune: "The Battle of Ivry
Man for His Own Hand; Being a Campaign Anthem. Air—*Jerusalem
the Golden.*" Accompanying is a brief note from Twain to his old
friend, the Rev. Joseph Twichell of Hartford, Conn. (envelope
postmarked New York City, Jan. 27, 1907):

Dear Joe:
  All the periodicals have refused this poem—ever since
election day.
  Get Charley Clark to put it in the *Courant.*

With love,
Mark.

One observes that Twain wanted his poetic effusions to be published or at least printed, and did not want them to lie around in
dusty drawers for years as *"1601"* had done, after also being sent to
Twichell. Much more important autobiographically are the two
Rubáiyát stanzas by Twain, beginning "A Weaver's Beam," and
lamenting his sexual impotence at date unknown. This was a theme
that had clearly tormented him a long time, and except for the
sardonic pun, "The Penis mightier than the Sword"—certainly its
best line—there is nothing humorous about this stark self-unveiling,
which encompasses in eight devastating lines Twain's private
tragedy: certainly the most significant lines he ever wrote. They
apparently form part of an extended imitation of the *Rubáiyát*
(unpublished: in the Mark Twain Papers at the University of California) reciting all the infirmities of old age, and written by Twain at
Sanna, Sweden, in September 1899: then retouched by him in 1906

·4·

when he was seventy. But even this advanced date, and the combination with other infirmities of age, cannot reduce the terrible impact of these two stanzas as autobiography. They are printed below for the first time.

Twain had already made impotence the closing point or punchline of "*1601*," written in 1876 when he was only forty-one years old. He also touches upon the matter lightly in "The Address to the Stomach Club" in 1879, and makes an elaborately symbolized reference to it in a tall tale concerning a turkey-gobbler that hatched a porcelain egg into a teapot without a spout, in his *Autobiography* at date May 30th, 1907, when his career was coming to an end in a blaze of pessimism and anti-religious mockery. It is evident that Twain here identified himself flatly with the male-motherhood turkey. What is more important is that he also seems to have thought of himself as the teapot without a spout. (See the full anecdote in *Mark Twain in Eruption*, edited by Bernard De Voto, 1940, page 23; and in my own *Rationale of the Dirty Joke: Second Series*, "*No Laughing Matter*," 1975, page 591, in the context of "Symbolic Castrations.")

There is also a long, non-humorous discussion of female appetite and male impotence in Letter VIII, in connection with sexual temperament and Christian morality, in Twain's *Letters from the Earth* (New York, 1962), probably a main reason why this posthumous volume was withheld from publication by Twain's heirs for more than fifty years after his death, though edited by Bernard De Voto and "ready for the printer" in 1939. Finally, Twain makes an unequivocal statement as to his own impotence as the fifth and closing numbered point in the "Mammoth Cod" speech, almost certainly written (as will be shown below) in March 1902, when he was sixty-six.

It may be suspected that Twain's much-lamented impotence was in part imaginary, as were some of the other masochistic and hypochondriacal complaints that made him take to his bed and wear only white daytime clothing—compare *Huckleberry Finn*, chapter 18—throughout the final years of his life. Perhaps what he had really been suffering from the whole while was the mere "married man's rust" of overfaithful husbands in need of a change of sexual diet, but loved his wife too much or was too intimidated by her to try. As in the bitter folk-epigram or proverb, not by Twain but worthy of him: *"A husband is a lover with the nerve removed."* Again, Letter VIII of *Letters from the Earth*, written in 1909, the year before Twain's death, is of obvious autobiographical import:

> During twenty-three days in every month . . . from the time a woman is seven years old till she dies of old age, she is ready for action, and *competent*. As competent as the candle-stick is to receive the candle. Competent every day, competent every night. Also, she *wants* that candle—yearns for it, longs for it, hankers after it, as commanded by the law of God in her heart.
>
> But man is only briefly competent; and only then in the moderate measure applicable to the word in *his* sex's case. He is competent from the age of sixteen or seventeen thenceforward for thirty-five years. After fifty his performance is of poor quality, the intervals between are wide, and its satisfactions of no great value to either party; whereas his great-grandmother is as good as new. There is nothing the matter with her plant. Her candlestick is as firm as ever, whereas his candle is increasingly softened and weakened by the weather of age, as the years go by, until at last it can no longer stand, and is mournfully laid to rest in the hope of a blessed resurrection which is never to come.

That certainly lays it on the line, and also seems to be dating the onset of Twain's marital impotence about his fiftieth year (1885: the year of *Huckleberry Finn*), which is far too early for the normal physiological impotence of old age. Twain must also have suffered an unpleasant shock then, perhaps connected, from the defacing of one of the illustrations in *Huckleberry Finn* by a disgruntled or facetious printer, giving Uncle Silas a large and prominent erection! (The entire first edition had to be withdrawn, and this illustration replaced.) It is also illuminating to compare here Twain's frankly masochistic revelation in "My First Lie," in which he describes how, as a young boy, he tried to get his mother to *stick pins into him*, on some cockamammy subterfuge about pretending to have been hypnotized—also a standard masochistic delight.

In *No Laughing Matter* (Rationale of the Dirty Joke: Second Series, 1975) pages 237 and 290-92, I have developed at some length the implications of a relevant passage from Freud showing how Oedipal conflicts and classical masochism of this type will generally lead to sexual impotence and other hypochondriacal complaints, when the mother-figure the man eventually marries and submits to becomes identified too clearly in his unconscious mind with the sexually-forbidden mother. Howard Teichmann's "intimate portrait," *George S. Kaufman* (New York, 1972) at pages 45, 157-80 and especially significantly pages 329-30, presents a classic case of this kind, being also that of a famous humorist. The simplest approach to such a problem would first be sexual REST, possibly for a protracted period, as in Twain's burlesque "The Appetite Cure" story, which sets the matter symbolically on its head, under the aspect of a cure of the jaded appetite for food. As with much that Twain wrote, this has to be read with the mathematical symbols correctly cancelled out, and the expurgations filled in.

Ultimately, when a widower in his seventies, Twain became a shameless chaser and collector of little girls, in the style of Lewis Carroll earlier—anyone from about eleven to seventeen would do—though apparently not for conscious sexual purposes. (See Prof. Hamlin Hill's lacerating biographical study of Twain's last ten years, *Mark Twain: God's Fool*, 1973, pages xxvii, 127-28, 195, and 260-61.) Again, the "Dirty Old Man" syndrome typical of impotence, as with King David and Abishag in *1 Kings*, i. 1-4.

Twain's affectation of pure white clothing in his last years —explained as mere ostentation, and fear of "dirt"—and his compulsive washing of his then-white hair, also clearly indicate almost conscious feelings of guilt, though probably for mere imaginings. As will be seen, Twain tries for some sardonic humor at the opening of the "Mammoth Cod" speech, as to having his bawdy poetry "sung by hundreds of sweet, guileless children." This rather puts out of the question any unconsciousness of the implications of the "Angel-Fish Aquarium" or harem of underage girls with whom he surrounded himself in his last years. Even more plainly, in the "Ashcroft-Lyon" document, the last longhand manuscript written by Twain, during 1909, he expresses his dissatisfaction with the sexual charms of his former secretary, Isabel Lyon, who had frankly set her cap for him after the death of his wife. Twain says flatly (as quoted in full context by Hamlin Hill, pages 230-31):

> Howells, I could not go to bed with Miss Lyon, I would rather have a waxwork. [She was] an old, old virgin, and juiceless, whereas my passion was for the other kind.

And yet, there remains a very real doubt. Perhaps the impotence that tormented Twain for so many decades was only the physical counterpart or expression of his own self-achieved literary castration, like that of his penultimate image on the subject: the spoutless teapot. For the truth about Twain's unexpurgated writings, and why they are so few in number despite his obvious delight in the genre (consider "*1601*," and the hilarious digression on "pissing against the wall," in *Letters from the Earth*, x), is that even before his marriage Twain had placed himself, with self-dedicated masochism of the social if not physical type, under the tutelage of an earlier surrogate-mother, Mary Mason Fairbanks, who was to "refine" both Twain's person and his prose. The job his wife, Olivia Langdon, undertook to do later. His wife's letter to him, quoted by Prof. Hill, pages 41-42, overwhelming Twain with demonstrations of love to force his feet back on the profitable and elegant literary path of *The Prince and the Pauper*, *Joan of Arc*, and *A Connecticut Yankee*, is particularly significant. He had also another literary adviser and castrator always in the offing, William Dean Howells, a success-minded magazine editor and second-rate novelist of the period, not worth wiping Twain's shoes on.

Not until late in the 1890's and thereafter, when Twain finally erupted into the then-unpublishable anger and pessimism that mark all his last work—doubtless his reaction to the realization of having wasted himself for decades, first clearly expressed in the bitter *Tragedy of Pudd'nhead Wilson* in 1894—did he finally throw off this unpleasantly whole-souled interest in hitching the Pegasus of his genius to a milk-wagon, or rather, as he himself phrased it, to cultivating "corn-pone" (conformity and cash). But by then it was too late, and he consigned to his increasingly large "unpublishable" file a considerable part of what he then wrote, such as *The Mysterious Stranger* (of which he actually destroyed over one hundred pages in

1905: see Hill, page 111) and *Letters from the Earth* in 1909, when this did not profitably fit into his long-outgrown pose as merely a good-natured humorist. A pose wholly exploded in Justin Kaplan's sensitive biography, *Mr. Clemens and Mark Twain* (New York, 1966). Though obviously Twain himself had done his damndest to destroy his legend as a parlor humorist by his anti-imperialist and anti-religious essays after 1902, such as the attacks on King Leopold, Czar Nicholas, the missionaries, and Mary Baker Eddy!

The brief, undated poem avowing Twain's sexual impotence, "A Weaver's Beam," has had a singular history. A copy was sent to me over thirty years ago for my work on erotic balladry, in progress, by Mr. George Frederick Gundelfinger, of Sewickley, Pennsylvania, a Yale alumnus decades ahead of his time, who had the curious habit of stuffing the mailboxes of the entire incoming freshman class at Yale, year after year, with pamphlets of his own composition on sexual hygiene. In particular one on the art—rather than the presumed dangers—of masturbation (compare Mark Twain's *"Some Remarks on the Science of Onanism,"* below), and similar items, to the scandal of the college authorities and the delectation of the Yale student body. For the whole story of Gundelfinger's Thirty Years' War with Yale, see his *The Storm of Protest "Which Will Never Come"* (Sewickley, Pa. 1944).

The one best line in any of Gundelfinger's publications was precisely "THE PENIS MIGHTIER THAN THE SWORD," which he proposed to publish as his paid advertisement or contribution to one of the student yearbooks. When I expressed my admiration for its witty typographical pun, he responded with a copy of the eight-line poem, as given below, leaving the erroneous implication that he was its author. In fact, Twain's original manuscript of the poem, almost identically, is now preserved in the Beinecke Collection at Yale. Gundelfinger's access to Twain's text remains obscure, as do many other details about this interesting personage, despite the cheerful abundance with which he supplied information. He told me, for example, that the Gundelfingers were an ancient and famous German family; that under the name of the magician Gundolf or Gandalf, an earlier Gundelfinger had done a social study of Shakespeare (which is a fact), and that the motto on his family coat-of-arms was "GUNDELFINGERUS ERECTUS NON CONSCIENTIUS," which may be more truth than poetry.

A WEAVER'S BEAM

A Weaver's Beam—the Handle of a Hoe,
A Bowsprit once—now thing of dough:
   A sorry Change, lamented oft with Tears
At Midnight by the Master of the Show.

Behold—the Penis mightier than the Sword,
That leapt from Sheath at any heating Word
   So long ago—now peaceful lies, and calm,
And dreams unmoved of ancient Conquests scored.

To complete the census of Mark Twain's erotic poetry, Franklin J. Meine also refers, in his excellent edition of "1601," to an unrecovered piece of bawdy verse written during Twain's California days, known as "The Doleful Ballad of the Neglected Lover," now lost. And finally, there is the four-stanza poem, beginning "I thank Thee for the Bull, O God!" opening the address to the Mammoth Cods club, below. One fragmentary stanza of this—or perhaps a folk "toast" that originally inspired Twain to write the rest?—has been in circulation in the Ozarks and elsewhere, at least since the 1920's. This stanza, in the form of a toast, is printed in Thomas R. Smith's anonymous folksong collection, *Immortalia* (Philadelphia [New York: Macy-Masius], 1927) page 123, as "The Bull:"

> Here's to the bull that roams the wood:
> He does the cows and heifers good;
> If it were not for his long, long rod,
> We'd not have any beef, by God!

Another one-stanza text, rather similar to that in *Immortalia*, is included in a manuscript collection of folk-poetry made by Dr. Weston LaBarre in the eastern United States, and especially at Yale, between 1939 and 1946. It ends with the first recovered allusion to the "cod," here referring however to the scrotum:

> If it were not for his dick and cod,
> What would we do for beef, by God!

A three-line version, also as a toast, is given in Vance Randolph's great unpublished collection, *Vulgar Rhymes from the Ozarks* (MS. 1954) No. 65, entitled "Here's to the Bull," and collected as a "manuscript from Mr. O. P.; Verona, Mo., July 20, 1951. He heard it on Horse Creek, in Stone County, Mo., about 1930." (This is less than two hundred miles from Hannibal, Missouri, where Twain grew up.) In this text the "dangling cod" is the main surviving element, twice repeated.

Meanwhile, Twain's possibly derivative little poem in four stanzas, the "Ballad of the Cod," had been printed for the first time by his bibliographer Merle Johnson in New York about 1920: two leaves in small octavo, in an edition of twenty copies—as though it were dynamite—including some line-illustrations. According to Jacob Blanck's *Bibliography of American Literature* (New Haven: Yale Univ. 1957) Vol. 2: page 224, no. 3531, another edition of unknown date was printed on a single slip of paper, before 1930, headed "Part of a Letter Written by Mark Twain;" and a third edition of nineteen copies marked *Second Edition*, was privately printed on pale yellow paper for the Hammer & Chisel Club, New York, 1937. Two copies of the printed text of the poem, as above, were repositoried by Johnson in the New York Public Library, Reference Division, former call-marks: 6-NBI and 6-NCW. As one of these is now reported "missing," the other has been wisely reshelved in the Rare Book Room. All three of these editions give the text of the poem only.

Johnson's text shows two superior variants from the form here-following: in stanza 2, "a meed of praise" for "a word of praise," and "mighty cod" for "Mammoth Cod"; and it adds an abbreviated version of the last four sentences of Twain's introductory note, as below. The original manuscript used by Johnson was believed to be repositoried in the Manuscript Department or Berg Collection of the New York Public Library, but cannot at present be found, and it is not known whether it contained all of the accompanying speech and the covering letters. However, the full text of Twain's speech and the letters, which are of great interest, have been unearthed since, and they are printed here complete, for the first time.

These were discovered in a short, typewritten commonplace-book, entitled *A Treasury of Erotic and Facetious Memorabilia*, apparently compiled about 1910 to 1915 by Henry N. Cary, a Chicago newspaper editor, and compiler also of a large sex-slang dictionary, *The Slang of Venery* (3 vols., mimeographed: Chicago, 1916), plagiarized in largest part from John S. Farmer & William Ernest

Henley's *Slang and Its Analogues* (London, 1890-1909). This type-script *Treasury* was bought by me in the early 1940's from a private bookdealer in Brooklyn, New York, who told me he had it from the well-known Chicago bookdealer, Ben Abramson, now deceased. I later returned this to him for repositorying in the Kinsey Library, Institute for Sex Research, Indiana University, where it is now preserved along with much other unpublished material compiled by Cary for his sex-slang dictionary. A set of printed galley-proofs of Cary's proposed bibliography to this work is in the New York Public Library's "uncatalogued" 3* Collection, suggesting that this Library may indeed have—or once had—the missing manuscript of Twain's Mammoth Cod address as well.

The Mammoth Cod poem (Twain says it is a song, but this need not detain us), the speech in which it is set, and the covering letters all appear in Cary's *Treasury of Erotic and Facetious Memorabilia* at folios 35-38, erroneously headed "LETTER BY PETROLEUM V. NASBY," this being the pseudonym of David Ross Locke, a minor humorist of the Civil War period. The purpose of this erroneous ascription, which was surely intentional, was perhaps to avoid embarrassing Twain who may still have been alive at the time. Twain died in 1910, at the age of seventy-four, and, as has been observed above, the Mammoth Cod speech, as its fifth and final point, maintains in several ways, with Twain's usual wry humor, that he was sexually impotent at the time it was written, which I believe can be shown to have been during the first weeks of March 1902.

There is a mystery as to the identity of the recipient of these undated letters and the poem, since both his name and Twain's have been omitted from the transcripts in Cary's *Treasury*, probably made about 1910. The following suggestion is purely speculative, but has at least the merit of offering a starting-point for solving the problem. The final letter makes quite clear that an ocean pleasure-trip on a boat sailing from Boston (home of the Mammoth Cods club?) and involving card-playing and the drinking of champagne, was to follow the delivery of the speech which was, if necessary, to be read *in absentia* for Twain. There was indeed one famous such card-playing trip that Twain made, in March and April 1902, with the monolithic Thomas B. Reed, Speaker of the House of Representatives, who had given up his position in April 1899 in disgust over America's first frankly imperialist war, against the Philippine Islands.

The historian Barbara W. Tuchman, in *The Proud Tower* (1966), closing her remarkable chapter on Reed, "End of a Dream," page 167, says concerning the period after his resignation from Congress, till his death in December 1902: "Living in New York, Reed formed a congenial companionship with Mark Twain, whose wit and turn of mind and sardonic outlook matched his own. They were guests together on board the yacht of the multi-trust capitalist Henry H. Rogers for a long cruise of which the epic legend survives that Reed won twenty-three poker hands in succession." Something like Bret Harte's "Heathen Chinee," no doubt. Twain reports in his log-notes—not without a certain pique—that this feat was achieved off the coast of Florida.

Aside from Henry H. Rogers, who was also Twain's literary plenipotentiary and investment counsellor, the guests were: Twain, Reed, W. T. Foote, Dr. C. C. Rice, Col. A. G. Paine, and Laurence Hutton, editor of *Harper's Magazine*. Most of these men had also been guests on an earlier cruise of Rogers' yacht, the *Kanawha*, which this time sailed for the Bahama Islands and the West Indies. If these were indeed the "Mammoth Cods," as seems likely, it should be observed

MARK TWAIN

that they were not young men. Twain was sixty-six, Reed was sixty-three, their host Rogers was sixty-two, and Hutton was apparently the baby of the lot, at fifty-nine. The purposes of the club seem to have been fishing (for cod), gambling, and drinking; also obviously with a certain penchant for bawdry, if Twain's speech is any sample. Except for the essential fishing, many clubs like this exist today in America. Those of college men and air and army officers are mostly devoted to the singing of bawdy songs and limericks. A bootleg transcript of some of the unexpurgated and aggressive prose delivered nowadays at the Friars Club stag luncheons in New York is given in Earl Wilson's *Show Business Laid Bare* (1974) pages 22-25. This is precisely in the tradition of the Twain speeches, though far more crude.

Twain's work from October 1901 to mid-1903 is dated from Riverdale (the later Toscanini mansion) at the upper end of New York City along the Hudson, and he was invited to the all-male cruise on the *Kanawha* early in March 1902. According to Albert Bigelow Paine's *Mark Twain: A Biography* (1912) III. 1162-63, Rogers addressed his guests charmingly as "Owners of the yacht," signing himself as "Their Guest." Twain telegraphed or planned to telegraph Rogers his acceptance as follows, and this should be compared with the opening note below (by an unknown hand, perhaps Cary's) as to "his regrets at not being able to be present . . . on an excursion." Also with the final covering letter, below, of very similar tone and subject. This telegram is given, from the draft, by Paine and in Twain's *Correspondence with Henry Huttleston Rogers*, edited by Lewis Leary (Berkeley, Cal.: University of California Press, 1969) pages 482-84, a work which does not of course include the "Mammoth Cod" letters.

H. H. Rogers, Fairhaven, Mass.

Can't get away this week. I have company here from tonight till middle of next week. Will *Kanawha* be sailing after that & can I go as Sunday-school superintendent at half rate? Answer and prepay.

Dr. Clemens

In fact, Twain left New York to catch the yacht on Thursday, March 13th—compare the reference to "Thursday night" in the final letter below—as his letters to his wife Olivia show.

It will be observed that the "Sunday-school superintendent" joke is identical with that at both the beginning and end of the speech. The clear implication is therefore that the letters and speech were sent to Henry H. Rogers, doubtless as host to the Mammoth Cods on their expedition on the water, in which case Rogers' business office was perhaps "the Store" modestly referred to. The situation is classic from the time of "Trimalchio's Banquet" in the *Satyricon* of Petronius (about 60 A.D.) to the mansions of Chicago today. The rich parvenu—Rogers and Rockefeller were among the first of the oil-millionaires—who invites the greatest writer-and-humorist of his time to the junket on his yacht, with the understanding that the writer will furnish a bawdy monologue to entertain the guests at the sailing-party. *Say something funny, Sam!* Whatever the case, this legendary cruise might well be the one the aging Twain is savoring in advance in the final letter, saying with evident sincerity: "I *do* want to go on that excursion; I want to play poker once again before I die, and to breathe the salt air out of the mouth of a champagne bottle and be wicked. I have been good too long."

G. Legman

THE MAMMOTH COD

[*A party of gentlemen in the East, who were particularly fond of codfishing, formed a club called "The Mammoth Cods." Nasby* [sic] *writes his regrets at not being able to be present with them on an excursion as follows:*]

Dear——,

Yours, inviting me to join the excursion of the "Mammoth Cods" on the 29th inst., is at hand. Of course, I thank you, for I know you only desire my good; but whether it will be for my good to always accept your invitations is a question. I have been led from the sweet simplicity of my ordinary life into questionable paths too often by accepting your invitations, not to make me pause and consider when I receive one. I do not understand the meaning of the title of your Association, but I presume it expresses a peculiar quality in the membership—that is to say, I presume it is an organization made up of gentlemen whom mistaken nature has endowed with private organs of a size superior to common mortals. The word "cod" is frequently used in ancient literature to signify penis, and I take it that you use it in that sense. In a little poem that I wrote for the instruction of children, I used the word in the same way. I give you a copy of it. I wrote it to show the youth of the country that animals do better by instinct than man does by reason, unless it is properly guided. I intended it for the Sunday Schools and when sung by hundreds of sweet, guileless children, it produces a very pretty effect.

THE MAMMOTH COD

I.

I thank Thee for the Bull, O God!
    Whene'er a steak I eat.
The working of his Mammoth Cod
    Is what gives us our meat!

II.

And for the ram a word of praise!
    He with his Mammoth Cod
Foundation for our mutton lays
    With every vigorous prod.

III.

And then the Boar, who, at his work,
    His hind hoofs fixed in sod,
Contented, packs the Embryo Pork,
    All with his Mammoth Cod!

IV.

Of beasts, man is the only one
    Created by our God,
Who purposely, and for mere fun,
    Plays with his Mammoth Cod!

I object to your Society for several reasons:

1st. I fail to see any special merit in penises of more than the usual size. What more can they achieve than the smaller ones? I have read history carefully, and I nowhere find it of record that the sires of

Washington, Bonaparte, Franklin, Julius Caesar, or any of the worthies whose names illuminate history, were especially developed; and as it is not a matter of history, it is fair to assume that they carried regular sizes. In this, as in everything else, quality is more to be considered than quantity. It is the searching, not the splitting weapon that is of use.

2nd. It is unfair for a set of men who are thus developed to arrogate to themselves, superiority. It is something they are not responsible for, except, indeed, they increase its size by means that no man should be proud of. In my green and salad days a lady whom I wickedly tried to overcome for months, finally yielded. In just eight days I had a penis, or as you term it, a "Cod" of a size that would have entitled me to admission to your Order, were you all as well hung as jackasses. Was I to put on airs because injection of Nitrate of Silver swelled that organ? Heaven forbid! On the contrary I wore sack-cloth and ashes, as soon as I could get it out of its sling, and was ashamed.

3rd. It is unscriptural. We are as we were made. Can any of you by taking thought add one cubit to his stature? [*Matthew*, vi. 27.] I have, at times, by taking thought added inches to this organ; but it was not a permanency, and should not therefore be counted.

4th. Largeness of this organ is proof positive that it has been cultivated. The blacksmith gets an enormous arm by constantly exercising that limb, and I suppose a man by constantly using his private member will increase the size of it. Membership in your Society is a confession of immorality.

5th. I never go where I am looked upon as an inferior. Having devoted myself all my life to pious study and meditation; having formed my delights, not in the fleeting and unsatisfactory pleasures of sexuality and debauchery, but in the calm pursuits of religion and other learning, I really don't know whether I have such a thing as a "Cod" about me. I know there is a conduit about my person which is useful in conveying the waste moisture of the system, and is therefore, I suppose, necessary, but that is the only use I have ever put it to, except the natural one of procreation. I may be excused for this, for it would be a shame to have the kind of man I am die out with myself. I would not inflict such an injury upon the world. As for what men of the world call pleasure, I have heard, accidentally, many names for it, but I know nothing about it, and care less. My recollection of it is, that while it was, perhaps, pleasant, it was so brief and transitory it was not worth my while to repeat; still there may be pleasure in it for those who are not wrapped up in mental pursuits, and who make a study of it. As a philosopher I would investigate it had I not more important matters in hand.

Dear——, I trust these reasons are sufficient for my not joining the expedition; still, as wicked as you are, and as much as you are given to the vain and transitory pleasures of this life, I trust you will have a good time. You cannot sin much on the water, and if you play I know you will lose your money and thus lessen your means of sinning when you get ashore. Go with the gay revellers and have what you call "a good time." While you are thus engaged think of me, busy in my translation of the New Testament, and varying the monotony of the labor with the preparation of my hymns for Children,—a sample of which I have sent you.

May the Lord (?) Bless you,

Faithfully,

————

* * * * * *

·21·

Dear ——,

I enclose a letter which will perhaps answer your purpose. It is not very witty nor very wise, but, if read when the audience is half drunk, may answer. Write and tell me if I take the boat Thursday night, do I get in Boston in time to join the expedition? I am going to be there if possible, but I don't want to leave here until Thursday night, and I want to go by the boat. Write me all about it and where shall I come? Shall I have to rush straight to the boat, or will I have time to come to the Store and go with you like a Christian. Let me know about this at once. I am anxious to come, and shall if it be possible. May the Lord (?) Bless you, and keep you, and watch over you. You are too wicked to die, and too good to live. I *do* want to go on that excursion; I want to play poker once again before I die, and to breathe the salt air out of the mouth of a champagne bottle and be wicked. I have been good too long.

Truly,

——

THE STOMACH CLUB

SOME REMARKS ON THE SCIENCE OF ONANISM

MY gifted predecessor has warned you against the "social evil—adultery." In his able paper he exhausted that subject; he left absolutely nothing to be said on it. But I will continue his good work in the cause of morality by cautioning you against that species of recreation called self-abuse—to which I perceive you are too much addicted. All great writers upon health and morals, both ancient and modern, have struggled with this stately subject; this shows its dignity and importance. Some of these writers have taken one side, some the other. Homer in the second book of the *Iliad*, says with fine enthusiasm, "Give me masturbation or give me death!" Caesar, in his *Commentaries*, says, "To the lonely it is company; to the forsaken it is a friend; to the aged and to the impotent it is a benefactor; they that are pennyless are yet rich, in that they still have this majestic diversion." In another place this experienced observer has said, "There are times when I prefer it to sodomy."

Robinson Crusoe says, "I cannot describe what I owe to this gentle art." Queen Elizabeth said, "It is the bulwark of Virginity." Cetewayo, the Zulu hero, remarked, "A jerk in the hand is worth two in the bush." The immortal Franklin has said, "Masturbation is the mother of invention." He also said, "Masturbation is the best policy." Michelangelo and all the other old masters—Old Masters, I will remark, is an abbreviation, a contraction—have used similar

·23·

language. Michelangelo said to Pope Julius II, "Self-negation is noble, self-culture is beneficent, self-possession is manly, but to the truly grand and inspiring soul they are poor and tame compared to self-abuse." Mr. Brown, here, in one of his latest and most graceful poems refers to it in an eloquent line which is destined to live to the end of time—"None know it but to love it, None name it but to praise." [*Actually by FitzGreene Halleck.*—ED.]

Such are the utterances of the most illustrious of the masters of this renowned science, and apologists for it. The name of those who decry it and oppose it, is legion; they have made strong arguments and uttered bitter speeches against it—but there is not room to repeat them here, in much detail. Brigham Young, an expert of incontestable authority, said, "As compared with the other thing, it is the difference between the lightning bug and lightning." Solomon said, "There is nothing to recommend it but its cheapness." Galen said, "It is shameful to degrade to such bestial uses that grand limb, that formidable member, which we votaries of science dub the Major Maxillary—when they dub it at all—which is seldom. It would be better to decapitate the Major than to use him so. It would be better to amputate the *os frontis* than to put it to such a use." The great statistician, Smith, in his report to Parliament, says, "In my opinion more children have been wasted in this way than in any other."

It cannot be denied that the high antiquity of this art entitles it to our respect; but at the same time I think that its harmfulness demands our condemnation. Mr. Darwin was grieved to feel obliged to give up his theory that the monkey was the connecting link between man and the lower animals. I think he was too hasty. The monkey is the only animal, except man, that practices this science; hence he is our brother; there is a bond of sympathy and relationship between us.

Give this ingenious animal an audience of the proper kind, and he will straightway put aside his other affairs and take a whet; and you will see by his contortions and his ecstatic expression that he takes an intelligent and human interest in his performance.

The signs of excessive indulgence in this destructive pastime are easily detectible. They are these: A disposition to eat, to drink, to smoke, to meet together convivially, to laugh, to joke, and to tell indelicate stories — and mainly, a yearning to paint pictures. [*A reference to Twain's friend, the painter Edwin Abbey, a member of the Stomach Club.* — ED.] The results of the habit are: loss of memory, loss of virility, loss of cheerfulness, loss of hopefulness, loss of character, and loss of progeny. Of all the various kinds of sexual intercourse, this has least to recommend it. As an amusement, it is too fleeting; as an occupation, it is too wearing; as a public exhibition, there is no money in it. It is unsuited to the drawing-room, and in the most cultured society it has long since been banished from the social board. It has at last, in our day of progress and improvement, been degraded to brotherhood with flatulence — among the best bred these two arts are now indulged in only in private — though by consent of the whole company, when only males are present, it is still permissible, in good society, to remove the embargo upon the fundamental sigh.

PRINTED 1976 FOR MALEDICTA, INC.
MILWAUKEE, WISCONSIN